GROUNDHOG DAY

To Leezie Borden and M.K. Kroeger -B.L.

Copyright © 2000 by Betsy Lewin.
All rights reserved. Published by Scholastic Inc.
SCHOLASTIC, SCHOLASTIC READER, and associated logos
are trademarks and/or registered trademarks of Scholastic Inc.

Library of Congress Cataloging-in-Publication Data

Lewin, Betsy, author, illustrator.
Groundhog Day / by Betsy Lewin.
pages cm
Originally published: New York : Scholastic, 2000.
Summary: An incident on Groundhog Day reveals the true relationship
between Phil the groundhog and his shadow.
ISBN 0-545-79968-6 (pbk.) — ISBN 0-545-80162-1 (ebook) — ISBN 0-545-80163-X (eba ebook)
1. Groundhog Day—Juvenile fiction. 2. Woodchuck—Fiction. (1. Groundhog Day—Fiction.
2. Woodchuck—Fiction. 3. Shadows—Fiction.) I. Title.
PZ7.L58417Gr 2015
(E)—dc23
2014032491

ISBN 978-0-545-79968-3 (pbk.)/ ISBN 978-0-545-80162-1 (ebook)/ ISBN 978-0-545-80163-8 (eba ebook)

12 11 10 9 8 7 6 4 3 2 1   15 16 17 18 19 20/0

Printed in the U.S.A.   40
This edition first printing, January 2015

GROUNDHOG DAY

PHIL

by Betsy Lewin

SCHOLASTIC INC.

It's February 2nd, Groundhog Day.

Everyone is waiting for Phil,
the groundhog, to wake up
and come out of his burrow.

If it's cloudy, Phil won't see his shadow, and he will stay outside. That means spring will come soon.

If it's sunny, Phil will see his shadow. He will go back inside his burrow, and there will be six more weeks of winter.

But Phil is still asleep
in his dark, warm bed.

Suddenly, Phil is lifted up,
high in the air.

Everyone cheers!

Then, Phil is on
the cold ground.
He takes a few steps
and looks around.

No shadow.

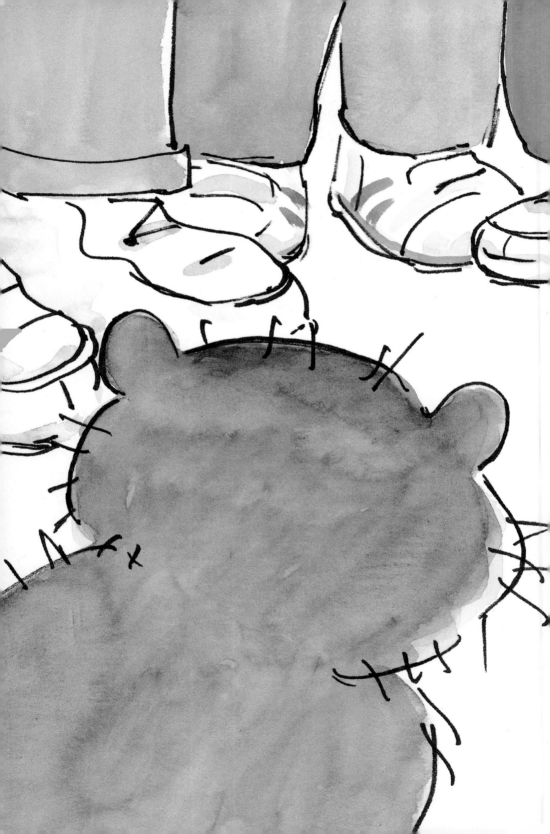

He sees lots and lots
of feet, but no shadow.

He looks up and sees
a cold, gray sky,
but no shadow.

The crowd shouts, "Hooray!
Phil does not see his shadow.
Spring is on the way!"

Phil hears a big "click!"
A light flashes.
The light makes a shadow!

"Eek!" squeaks Phil.
He dives back into his burrow.

All these years, people thought
it was the weather.
Now we know the truth.
Phil is afraid of his own shadow!